Bought Love Is A Salaried Position

Steven Saus

Alliteration Ink | Dayton

Published by
Alliteration Ink
PO Box 20598
Dayton, OH 45420
alliterationink.com

Bought Love Is A Salaried Position
ISBN 13: 978-0-9840065-1-9
ISBN 10: 0984006516

March 2012

10 9 8 7 6 5 4 3 2 1

Table of Contents

Bought Love Is A Salaried Position

Foreword

I don't write poetry. I tell myself that, and reams of bad drunken verse demonstrate that. But these pages are how I wrote for more than two decades. These words live somewhere between a poem and a short story. They are paragraphs and scenes of imaginary lives; bursts of personal exorcism. I wrote until I had evicted them from my mind in unconscious symbol and simplistic words.

Some of these stories date to last century, collected in photocopied journals that I mailed to surprised friends and mystified relatives. My life was changing then, my writing was changing then. They were flash fiction before flash fiction.

It's time these words take a little rest. My life has changed again, and it's time to close one chapter as I begin a new one. The leaves spiral downward at the height of their color, and for a minute we stop and notice.

My life is changing once more. It is only appropriate that I collect these again. A few things have been left out. A few things have been edited slightly. A few things have been added. But this collection started as history.

After we stop and notice the leaves, we must keep walking.

Will you walk with me?

Steven Saus

March 2012, Dayton

Pure

A clean sheet of paper
Pristine in its purity
Wasted by words worth nothing
For they destroy that pure paper
That they praise.

Untitled Poem

He looks up at me, little strange thing,
a carnival mirror stunted and warped,
vaguely recognizable as coming from me,
frowning, wondering why I
haven't learned from the songs,
haven't been taught by poems,
remain unenlightened by stories.
Why my apologies and regrets come much, much too late,
after the movers have taken his painful baggage to the
Dream-King's home and woven them into recurring nighttime
terrors.

Sometimes I try to explain -
halting words trying to hold liquid concepts in porous hands
but it is never really enough.
He looks up at me, says I love you.
Bangkick reflex; I say I love you too.

At night I cry.

The Pie Is A Lie

"I'm tired of only getting the scraps and leavings of your affection." She threw his dessert on the table hard enough for the saucer to ring.

He looked up from his laptop, brow furrowed. "That's not pie. What is that?"

"Leftovers," she said. "It's symbolic."

"Feh." He pushed the plate away, turning back to his computer.

She blurred into motion, knocking him and the laptop to the ground, dinner's steak knife dripping with A1 at his throat.

"You've been starving me of affection," she said. The knife pressed into his skin. "And I'm hungry."

He didn't feel the first bite.

Six Shooter

Peter was ten when he first noticed that his favorite six-shooter didn't have a hammer.

It was Bobby Shomaker's fault, really. He'd shown up at the front door decked out in his bandanna and cowboy hat, the rim half-blocking the sharp Texas sun. Peter was grabbing his own hat and six-shooter even as his mother yelled upstairs for him.

The two kids ran wild for a few minutes, screaming as they tore through the lawns of their neighborhood, chasing each other to the dry streambed they called their own.

"Lookit this, Peter," Bobby said, withdrawing the gleaming silver of the cap gun. "My parents bought it for me yesterday."

Peter solemnly accepted the weapon, his eyes widening in delight as the sun glinted off the metal. He loving caressed the simulated mother-of-pearl handle, his finger delicately tracing the stamp of "Cowboy Bob", complete with crossed lassoes. Bobby reclaimed his prize, showing Peter how to fire off caps with it.

They tasted their anticipation as Bobby dry-fired it several times, hearing the sharp click of metal on metal. As the boys spent the afternoon exploding small amounts of gunpowder and frightening birds, Peter occasionally stole glances at his weapon, dingy, hammerless, and harmless in the dirt.

When Peter returned home, he went straight to his room, leaving the six-shooter abandoned on the living room floor.

He didn't talk to his parents for the rest of the night.

Elephants Led To Water

"No," Sandra said, as the small grey animal on the floor trumpeted. She stalked past, through the kitchen toward their son's room.

"You like elephants," Andrew said. "Remember, that clown who made you the balloon elephant?" He picked up the pachyderm. "This one's about the same size, honey."

She called upstairs to their son. "James! Time to go to come home."

"You could play with the elephant," Andrew said. "Or James could, while we talked."

Their son careened down the stairs and took Sandra's hand. They went outside, slamming the door behind them.

Andrew petted the elephant. It trumpeted quietly.

Lifetune

Imagine what it's like for her, the gap-toothed thrusting, she's a twenty dollar masturbation aid - lifelike! ribbed for your pleasure! - but it's just too different.

Tender cries just don't do it anymore as he digs, digs deep in her mind, trying to sift the chaff for the part he wants, the part he needs, but she doesn't dare whimper, doesn't dare show the fear; he doesn't dare leave marks, polaroidable evidence as he shudders and she sighs, a brief respite won.

I'll just change my head, she says, this one's starting to wear down, kick back the beer, wait for the broken record - the only one she owns - to come home again.

Drunk, bold, try to break the needle before it pierces, playing the song yet again, scraping the worn grooves on her soul, untender cry played through aging gramophone.

There is a point, she tells me. It's usually buried in my heart.

Lease Agreement

Anton dropped the drained husk. "My first real kill," he whispered. The longing, a lonely emptiness he'd never really noticed had vanished, filled with the pulsing warmth of blood.

Kelenthia slid behind him, raven hair brushing his ear. "You did well, my fledgling," she said. Her fangs sank into his neck. It was not the willing surrender of the Change. She forced herself into him, and took, and took, and took.

She left him lying there, the gnawing emptiness back in his gut.

"The extra, the passion, the pleasure belongs to me," she'd said. "Consider it rent on your afterlife."

Virgin

You never forget the first time.

I was curiously detached, shriekingly aware of the passion, the simple brutality of it, but it simply washed right through me, leaving my intellect clean in its wake.

My muscles contracted, arcing my back into the air, clutching desperately at her soft flesh. I'm ashamed to admit it now, but I was scared, my vision tunneled to her white face as the moans escaped my throat. Her wide eyes swallowed me. My nails dug through her blouse and she gasped, her comforting forsaken for a moment, the rivulets of blood soaking into the tatters of her blouse.

Fascination with these things, the electric nerves chattering to each other across the network of my brain. Never had I felt my body like this - out of control, drawn out from one second to the next, puppet tied to the strings of an unknown master.

As her concern for me finally transformed into fear, I blacked out.

When I awoke, only minutes later, my face was buried in the steaming pit of her gut, my fur matted with her blood.

It does not taste anything like chicken.

Brain Food

"Jonathan, you can't talk about UFOs if you want to get into Mensa." Abigail ignored his tight knuckles gripping the steering wheel. "You're a smart guy, but they won't get it."

"You bet they won't get it," he snorted. "Smartest people in the world and they're UFO deniers." He swerved into the library parking lot. "We're finally here."

"Look," Abigail said, "I'll take you to a nice restaurant for our next date."

As the humans walked inside, Bleargh looked up from the monitor to Zooptif. "A brain buffet!" it said, "What a romantic date!"

The saucer landed on the roof.

Ultimate Wrestling

The camera shook when the wrestler hit the mat in a clumsy break-fall, shaking the picture on the television imperceptibly amid the sonic vibrations of a distant bomb. Vlasdec thought of the trite cliches of the footsteps of giants, then reflected that it might just be true - in a warped Asgardian sensibility of the damned.

His wife's cooled head lay in his lap; his right hand absently stroking her dark hair as the overweight men pretended to fight on the television. The chugchugchug of the small gasoline generator was a steady beat against the arrhythmic pounding of the blasts. Angelica's videotapes clattered from a shelf to the floor - hours of the recorded ritual dance of the wrestling shows - underdog and champion, a brief skirmish, the champ pinned for one, two - then the amazing surprise recovery choreographed to the exacting standards of pay-per-view television, and the defeat of evil, the champ beaming to the adoration and money of his fans.

He had passed by the graveyard yesterday while scavenging for food, discovering that a bomb had struck the holy land, churning the earth and shallow hastily-dug graves. He could not find Angelica's tombstone, nor a piece he could identify as her, so he left, the stench caressing his clothes ever since.

Vlasdec sat in his easy chair, staring at his dead wife's gorgeous eyes being eaten by the flies as the bombs drew nearer, waiting for the ref to finally count to three, even though it wasn't written in the script like that.

Eventually the ref did.

Any Given Evening For A Dark Superhero

I pull off the back door of the paddywagon. A cop flies out too, thumping hard on the concrete. The supervillain's last henchman is ziptied to the seat. Another officer looks back through the window. My exoskeleton smashes through reinforced glass and cop skull alike.

"I was wonderin' when we'd get sprung," the henchman says.

My head swivels toward him. "Who hired your boss?" The ectoplasm from the villain's defeat still smears across the San Matias sky.

"Wha? I dunno."

"Damn." I turn to leave.

"I thought you were getting' me out?"

"Psyche," I say, and tear out his spleen.

Two by Two

Contrary to written records, Noah's family did most of the species gathering. The animals milled in pens all around Noah's farm while he finished the ark.

"Advanced degree in genetics," Noah said, "and the Lord has me sawing wood. You'd think He likes carpenters or something."

Upon finishing, Noah realized how little space was inside the ark. "Lord," he said as the rain began to fall, "there's only room for two of each animal. The genetic bottleneck will -"

The flash and boom of an atomic explosion echoed from the distance.

"Don't worry about it," said the Lord. "There'll be mutations."

Condiments

She doesn't believe me.

Somehow her eyes tell me - even though eyes cannot really change (I know this, another part of the useless trivia of life). Even without her withdrawn body and uncomfortable speech I could simply look at her listening jelly orbs to see her soul judging by her impressions, her cliches, instead of by me.

She agrees as so many do - words so frequently lied that no-one believes them anymore - and there's still no other way to say them. She doesn't believe me. Irised jelly tells me, and I prefer jam.

Fishing

I think I would have screamed if it had been night.

Pinpricks, and my mind was loosed, back in time. I walk into this room, fighting against myself, tearing her picture down from the mantle. I enter my house for the first time in weeks, realizing it is much too quiet and empty. I step off the plane, briefcase in hand, and attempt to hail a taxi at the same time as two hundred people from my plane. I try to hint to the rather large lady beside me that, no, I don't wish to talk during the four hour long flight, my ears are refusing to pop and I'm in a rather cross mood. The conference ends, and we all leave, having talked and drank too much, getting very little done, as is the way with conferences. Two weeks worth of blurry nights. Another plane - the seat beside me this time mercifully empty, with only an inane film to keep me company. Kissing her good-bye at the airport, hugging my son (just old enough to not want to be kissed anymore).

They come faster, too fast to recognize them all. Holding the squalling creature in my arms after a sleepless night at the hospital, a brief flash of tuxedos and dresses - a preacher presiding. A night in a motel because the dorms won't allow female visitors overnight, the first time I saw her - in someone else's arms, obviously unhappy, and the radiance which illuminated her face when she saw me. Blue and red robes as we proceeded in, finally adults in everyone's eyes, the piece of paper secondary to the fact that we did it after all, fuck you very much, sitting in a smoky house as curiosity finally got the better of me, spending the rest of the night staring at people's faces and seeing the beauty underneath.

Faster now, but perfectly clear. Every memory crisp and new, even though I could not have found them on my own. Coming into home, breaking my wrist as I got tagged out, and more upset about being out than my wrist.

Being spanked for picking up a package of gum at the store and putting it in my pocket - my parents discovering when they found me chewing my illicit treasure.

Suckling at my mother's breast.

A bright flash of light.

Blackness.

Suddenly we were separate, his wise eyes turning towards me between his curled black locks. He took his fingernail and sliced an expert incision in the olive skin of his wrist - my mouth surrounding it, sealing it.

Faster than mine his memories came - watching me, the hunt repeated endless times for centuries again and again without end, the legions that had fallen before Him. Flashes of both day and night - the legend disproved - an invention of Man to keep fear of Him away. He was my Universe as I drank deep of Him, traveling farther back; women in petticoats, then men in wigs.

Barbarians painting their faces blue, blond marauders following their own codes of honor. Civilization rising and falling. Rome. Caesars are flashes in His memory. Languages ebb and flow like a tide, fashions flash by, lightning bolts of styles. And then the flow of his life begins to slow.

A small room with His friends, not overly long after His birth, they not expecting anything more than a simple ritual meal. As He devoured each of them, He offered Himself in return, an orgy of blood and unholy life.

Drink of me, that you may live.

He pushed me away from His wrist, and I collapsed, staring up at His beautiful face. Then He took my hand, and we leapt from the window to become fishers of men.

Absorbing

When amoebas absorbs something, they cannot help but have that which they absorbs become part of themselves - perhaps transmuted somewhat, but they have become that which they has absorbed as surely as that which was absorbed have become the amoebas.

The same applies to reading.

Balloon Animal

"I don't want to go on the stupid ride." Sarah put her small fists on her hips, staring at her father.

The spin-and-puke (or whatever) sang the same shrill tune as the neighborhood ice cream truck. "Okay," her father said. "How about a balloon animal?" A nearby mime, hearing him, wheeled his tank and deflated balloons closer.

"I want Spot to be alive again," Sarah wailed, tears streaking her dusty face.

The mime lifted a finger and went to work. In moments, he presented Sarah with the inflated dog.

She looked unimpressed, until it licked her and wagged its tail.

Drinking Beer With God

God came to me in a dream last night.

I had been really drunk at Susan's party - I remember the wobbling of my steps, the spinning in my skull. Susan kissing me good night a little more thoroughly than a married woman should, and me not giving a damn.

The next thing remembered is my pillow. Then God was there.

He wasn't the lightning-bearded horror of Revelations, or the wise old grandfather. Just a guy, about five-ten, with a bit of a gut, receding hairline, and perfect teeth. Immaculate teeth. I remember thinking how odd it was that I cared about this guy's teeth. I never was a tooth person before.

And he was naked. But that didn't matter. For some reason I was fixated on his perfect gleaming teeth. Despite the beer gut and receding hairline, I somehow knew it was God. Maybe it was the teeth, but I doubt it.

I was suddenly afraid, my still-drunk brain reeling with the memories of all the times I'd said: "Well, if God were here, I'd ask Him why it was that way."

Suddenly I was ashamed of all those times. And then God told me why anyway.

We traveled that night, in my dreams. Across the Universe, through the world. I saw DNA up close and personal, saw a race of aliens discovering the usefulness of fire. And it all finally made sense.

I shook God's hand (getting a nasty shock from static electricity, which we had a nice laugh over), and invited him to have a beer with me sometime. It was about then that I woke up, sweating in my bed with the phone ringing at 3:47 am.

Susan was on the phone. Josh, a co-worker of ours, had tried to drive home and succeeded in wrapping his car around a telephone pole. He was in the emergency room at St. Mary's.

By the time I showed up, the doctor was telling everyone that Josh had just died. I started to tell Josh's wife about my dream to console her, to explain it, but the meaning of it all had blurred off into that place that forgotten dreams go. Josh's wife only cried harder.

I hope Josh got to drink a beer with God.

Eye of the Beholder

It was perfect. With the last few brush strokes he finished, looking at the eyelid he'd just perfected. It was a sweet paled pink, without eyeshadow - she didn't need it. Her long golden hair lay over her left shoulder as she sat on the white wicker chair. Her eyes were closed in her heart-shaped face, as if she were napping. He had decided on a white tank top (bulged by her firm breasts) and red shorts that came halfway to her knees.

He leaned forward, touching his brush to a knuckle, covering the blue discoloration that had peeked through.

He was proud of his work. He sat back and waited for her to rot.

It was Art.

Vacation

"One day into vacation," Beth said from the passenger seat.

"Yup." I kept my eyes on the road. The highway twisted through the forested hills.

She hit the button to open the sunroof. "We've only got six days left."

"At this rate, you'll burn the motor out before we have to return the car."

She laughed, deep and rich. She let her hair out of the ponytail. "Mark, did you really expect to just carpool to the beach?"

I thought about my cubemate who'd turned into the sexy woman beside me.

"I hope not," I said, and we both smiled.

Dead To Rights

Bob started giggling while we wheeled the gurney down the hospital hallway.

"This Is Not Funny," I said, biting off each word. The body - or client, as Bob called it - didn't smell, but I'd still put VapoRub under my nose. We clattered down the dark hallway toward the back exit.

"It's really nice of you," Bob said while he tried to stifle his giggles. "I mean, when Maggie called in at the last minute, I really needed someone to help me out here."

"It's not what you think. You're paying me."

"Sure," he said, "but not enough to be moving clients from the hospital morgue to the funeral home. And that's how I know you're a real friend."

"Don't."

"Because friends help you move, but real friends -"

I tried to focus on the corpse on the gurney, ignoring the sanity-blasting pun.

Never make friends with a mortician who moonlights as a stand-up comic.

Ant and Grasshopper

The ant worked all summer, gathering and storing food. The grasshopper squandered his time, laughing at the ant's industriousness.

Winter came, and the ant laughed at the starving grasshopper, shivering in the cold. So the grasshopper shot him and pissed on his grave.

Silence

The silence roars in my ears when they turn the monitors off. The tightly controlled medics emerge from the billowing curtain encased in spiritual shells, refusing to share, refusing to feel. Phone rings and I offer the ritually correct greeting to another - a remote bystander following us like a favorite soap opera. Stalling, sidestepping, buying some time for the others to wrestle demons into specimen bottles, under microscopes, to await detailed examination in the cold hard hours of early morning.

No bodybags are available - he's simply covered by a white sheet - wondering, hoping someone closed lifeless eyes in a final blink. The litterstraps are being fetched to a soundtrack of wails, ongoing, stretching out through time beyond the limits of human lungs, wavering cry of grief symbolic for those who cannot allow themselves to feel. Not yet. Strap him down tight, three straps - one two three - pull them tight so he won't slide away. Expect him to grunt, to complain they're too tight, mind pierced by the screaming alienness of a forever unmoving chest. Is he turning blue under the sheet? No, don't look.

He was moving when I first saw him, illuminated by alternating red and white lights. Struggling weakly and thrashing randomly, eyelids barely flickering. Blood had spilled like wine from his lips onto the pure white gurney sheet, flowing as we loaded him into the ambulance. They later tell me his heart was stopped when we arrived, but I didn't know it, shoving him through double doors yelling for help, surrounded by busy hurryscurry. Thinking back minutes to screaming sirens, roaring voice on the radio, weighing speed against flinging precious cargo from side to side in the back of the ambulance. Wishing we were closer, wishing we were there, adrenal time dilation making seconds eternity.

Changing the sheets on the gurney as behind the soft curtain ribs pop under compressions, plastic pushing air into unresponsive lungs. Try to be deaf as someone counts one two three four five breathe, sit at the desk unhearing as someone shouts "All clear!" and the muffled thump of voltage spasms. Direct the bewildered bystanders out of the area, bid them bide a while in uncomfortable seats just far enough away they cannot hear what I hear, cannot imagine what I imagine. Their own musings are bad enough.

Catch brief glimpses of swollen stomach and catheter and wonder at the lack of dignity at passing away this way, sweat dripping from determined workers on lifeless skin, shouted instructions and rushed movements about your unyielding form. Then the fear of blackness rises in my skull as it always does, and I make the phone call for the helicopter we all know will be far too late.

The litter sits on the clean gurney sheets, white wrapped about green pink and blue, with splashes of red. How tacky to clash when you're dead. Another drives the ambulance on the slow ride to the mortuary, rectangular box disappearing in perspective, turning a corner and out of my world - the strong smell of bleach pulling back to here and now, sponges and mops cleaning up after the storm. Walk back to my office, as useless now as when it began.

Out of sight, out of mind.

Yeah, right.

I never ask if they closed his eyes. I don't want to know.

Bedtime Story

Hansel shoved the girl up against the rough tree. "This ain't what I wanted."

"I don't have anything else," she whimpered, the red fabric of her cloak draping over her eyes. "Grandma just made the muffins. No cookies. No cake."

Hansel looked back toward his sister. "Whaddya think?"

Gretel walked out of the shadows. "I think we have a little girl who brought the wrong gift and now can't find her way home."

"Oh," Red Hood said, "all I have to do is take a left here and-"

Gretel drew her knife. "Not can't. She *won't* find her way home."

Moving

The bare wood floor speaks to her.

Standing, a tear falls from her face.

The flowered pattern of her dress flows in the breeze from the open windows. In her mind, the laugh of her children as they race across the living room; their father yelling for them to get out from in front of the television. A squeal and crying, legs bruised from the coffee table.

Nights alone with her husband, the candle flickering on his face, staring at the permanent sadness that etched his happiest mood, and knowing she loved him despite the burnt spaghetti.

Crying.

Laughing at the antics of a sitcom family, feeling the gnawing at the back of her head that they'd never be quite that happy. The movers drop a box upstairs, and she goes to see what part of her life they've destroyed.

Horror Stories

"So, you've had some stories published?" I hate the sound of my voice, old and quavering. Martha used to say I shoulda been in radio, but things just never worked out that way.

"Yes, grandpa." I still think of him as the boy, though he's older than I was when I married Martha. He's holding his book behind his back. "I've got a chapbook of short stories out."

"Oh," I say, and nod. "Good job." Damn voice wavers, makes me sound patronizing.

"Thanks, but they're... not really your speed." I see the knife and blood on the cover. "Thanks, though. Gotta go, grandpa."

I shake my head as he leaves, and try to decide between the Poppy Z. Brite novel or the Clive Barker one. Maybe I'll watch the Saw movies back to back again. I laugh a little to myself. I love them damn movies.

I hear the shouts outside, and hobble out to the porch. I shake my cane at the children, tell them to get the hell off my lawn, just as I always do. I walk back in and pick up the Saw DVD.

I need some new ideas for those damn kids on my lawn.

Untitled

As the storm abates around me, the thrashing trees resuming their eternal stillness, the moon shines cleanly through the breaking clouds, a silver spray of spring water upon the earth. Touching the rough illuminated bark of a broken plant, seeing the houses that have crushed under themselves, seeing the structures that stand, unreal illumination revealing modern ruins rapidly winding their way into rubble, a poetic portrait of the past in present portrayed against the inside of my eyes.

And I dread the dawn.

Pirates On Trial

The first defendant wore a "home taping is killing the music industry" shirt. "Plea?" I asked.

"Not guilty! Information wants to be free! "

"Innocent by reason of insanity." I said. "Ideological idiots. Next!"

The man had candles in his black beard. "Yarrr, me letter of mark from the Queen here says - "

"Dry him out in the drunk tank. He reeks of rum. Next!"

The third defendant wore a suit and tie. "I don't understand. I just ran the subprime CDO desk at an investment bank."

I leapt up. "Hang him. Hang him by the neck until he's dead, dead, dead!"

Signing

She's walking now, he's sure of it, walking toward him from the coffeeshop where she blended their souls on puree - she has to be walking this way. Her recorded words rip scars through his soul, laborious defenses useless against the subtle assault.

She appears in the doorway, his mental director screeching disapproval of her casual disregard of stage directions imagined countless times - she late, he unmoving, heartbeat pound her face sliding slamming into optics, desperate effort to say something, say something deep and profound, something, anything to let her know how she has helped you feel.

She smiles, and signs the book, and for a moment it is bliss.

Stage Directions

His fist thwacks into me, a sharp crack echoing off the restroom's metal walls. A sharp sunburst of pain as bones snap, a wet thud from tile meeting my flesh.

His boot slams into my ribs. I am airborne in a spinning sprawling shallow arc back to the ground. My blood spatters an abstract painting on the porcelain.

This would be cool in a movie.

I lay there for a moment. He turns to leave.

My hand grabs his ankle, draws him crashing to the ground. I rise over his half-conscious body.

"Brains," I say.

And then I feast.

Ten

The aliens told us to comply within ten hours, or face destruction. We had to give them all our men. Forever. As bull studs.

Some men showed up. The female aliens weren't ugly, after all. But a surprising percentage of men preferred life with thier families, thier lovers, thier jobs.

We thought we had time to prepare.

The countdown clock had two hours left when we noticed the translation was not ten hours, but "two hands of hours".

The aliens looked a lot like us.

They had four digits on each hand.

We heard lasers, held our spouses, and prayed.

Melt Into You

They lay motionless, the subtle poison he had introduced so eloquently to their drinks having paralyzed their voluntary muscles, leaving them alert, aware, and helpless.

"Ah, the sweet couple," he whispers as he sensously removes their clothes, fondling their skin with his fingertips, releasing more of their shining skin to the chilled air of the basement. Twin sets of eyes stare at him, glassy fear as he enfolds them into the other's arms, twining clay statues into an unnatural braid.

"Come, now, don't you want to share your love with each other?" he whispers, removing the surgical instruments from their cases, beginning to cut and sew, fusing their bodies in a surgical nightmare.

As the bodies gasped their last breaths, the dim light behind the eyes fading into nothingness, veins and arteries sharing the same blood, intestines hopelessly fused into a maze of flesh, skin stitched together with utmost care, he looks at them sadly, saying "I suppose there's a moral in this."

MLS

The main character looked at his female lead, and remarked, "This story's rather short, isn't it?"

She looked around bemusedly before responding.

"It is a bit cramped, after all," she said as she tried to flex one leg. "What can we do? This is absolutely horrid."

He placed his hand on his chin and frowned thoughtfully. "We are the main characters," he said, "and we could try using M.L.S. to expand a bit. We wouldn't have to take out a mortgage that way."

"M.L.S.?"

"MeaningLess Speech. A large part of the English language is made up of entirely unnecessary words and phrases. For example, I could have omitted the words 'A large part' and said "Most" instead, and completely removed the words "language" and "entirely'. Not to mention the articles, particles, and other debris that clutters up the language. If you have an ounce of intellect, you'd still get the meaning from the remaining words."

She shook her head confusedly after his speech. It was roomier, though. But her thoughts kept nagging her, so she went ahead and said it.

"But, if we don't need to say it, why are we saying it at all?"

The main character leaped to cover her mouth, but it was too late. The author ripped the page out of the typewriter and crumpled it before throwing it on the floor.

Small House on a City Street

A small house on a city street; unimpressive with stained and peeling paint. A rusted swingset sits in the backyard, rocking slowly back and forth in the autumn breeze. A leaf falls slowly, an elegant and graceful death, as beautiful as sad. The sun is a splash of orange paint on the hilly horizon, casting long shadows on the brown grass. The house echoes with the sound of a gerbil running in its wheel, a metallic racket attempting to fill the silence.

The living room looks out onto the empty street - tarred black and stained deep red. The carpet in the living room is lush and green, a verdant forest of nylon below the sky-blue walls. The television is on quietly; multicolored glows flooding the room as characters whisper to recorded laughter. Salty rain falls on the forest from the giant sitting over the toy car, just pulled from underneath a chair. She sobs as warm arms encircle her, pain turned into sounds agonizing to hear.

The arms leave after a while, to place momentos in cardboard boxes, taping them up with loving care, but the pain stays; a tear in the soul. Eventually it dog-ears itself back together, a poor substitute, but a beginning. She helps him pack their belongings: the lipstick, cologne, the bras and boxer shorts. The relics from Disneyland; faded Mickeys and broken Goofys smiling inanely despite their injuries.

She does not pack the child's room, leaving that to her husband as she starts to place boxes in the car.

As they drive, words try and fail to distract her, to keep her from picking at the scabs of her soul. She pays little attention to her dress, currently wedged firmly in the door, restraining her. Rows of two story houses stand at attention, a line of silent mourners. Turning down the winding streets, past foreboding monuments, gray spires and rectangles jutting from the hallowed earth, and the wound rips open in her soul, pouring forth the sorrow of a son lost while almost in reach.

Bearded face turns to try to help ease the sorrow as a yip pierces the air, and a thump vibrates through the seats. They stop the car and examine the broken fur bundle lying in the street, feeling the pain of similarity.

She grasps the slowly cooling body and holds it, her tears splashing softly on the black and white coat: the baptism it never had in life. Wind whisks around her as she carries it to the grave of her son, the earth still turned and raised above the ground. The body is arranged with honest care: two like souls in the afterlife.

She walks back to the car, taking care to not catch her dress in the door.

Stuffing

Angie arranged the dolls around the table. "Teatime!" she yelled.

Ellie held his denim trunk still as Angie poured imaginary tea. Bunny's plush ears did not twitch. R.A. (Esquire) flopped his stuffed head to the side, red yarn hair draping his shoulder.

"Raggedy." Angie stared at R.A. "Have some tea."

R.A. picked up the faded teacup. He glanced at Ann's severed head in the corner. She'd guessed wrong. He took a drink of pretend tea.

"Oolong," he guessed, mouth dry.

Angie smiled. "Yes!"

R.A. sighed in relief.

"From what country?" Angie asked.

R.A. swore Ann's button eyes winked in anticipation.

Waiting

The candles flicker in the slight breeze from the window as I wait for you to come.

When I open my eyes from the reverie spun by twisting music and soporific incense I see the clean white light of the moon spilling through the orange glow of the candles onto the wine red carpet plush beneath my feet.

Your picture is framed before me. Tracing your profile with a finger, a tear tracks its slow way down my cheek.

My eyes shut again, visions of your skin swimming behind them. Fingertips remembering the touch of your hair. Ears, listening hard for the sound of your voice. Holding my precious jewels of memory, fondling them obscenely, I wait for you to come.

A shiver up my bare back, but do not move to close the window. Dredge up the time we first met, not guilty about not knowing what you were wearing, just too entranced by your face, too engulfed by the beauty of your eyes to care, too entranced by the words you said. Remembering it vividly and not at all.

Pull my eyelids open with an effort of will to gaze at your picture again, my head slumped against my chest, covering my bare groin with the photograph. Just holding it, just staring, I wait for you to come.

Eyelids falling together again, not able to stop them.

I hear your voice outside, calling to me. Try to answer, but it is hard, so very hard.

But when you walk through the wall, I have the strength to take your hand.

Cabbage

The cabbages gained sentience on a Thursday.

They conquered the Earth by Saturday.

Some humans simply went mad, unable to deal with the vegetable voices in their supermarkets, in their stomachs. Other humans required more emphatic persuasion to submit.

A cabbage moving at high speed suffers little damage when impacting a human skull.

The skull is not so lucky.

That Sunday, mass funerals were held for the victims of coleslaw violence outside of every KFC. All countries, led by cabbage rulers, declared peace.

At least the world was finally in harmony.

Until the next Thursday, when the rutabagas started talking.

Profile of a Psychotic

Smell of fear drifts through air, mixes with liquor and vomit; urine a steady undercurrent of the whole. Soft patter of rain on a metal roof- hard patter of soled feet striking the ground. Shadows flit - specters avoiding light, the havens of the unscrupulous. Tweed jacket, fine cologne masking the baser scents. Snicksnick of hard leather against pavement. Rustle of movement, startled turn flaring the jacket, nothing seen. Rasping steel barely sounding, moonlight gleaming on metal as the leather soles resume the noisy chorus, the padding of following feet indistinct against the sound of the rain.

Brief warning: swift smell of goats, flashing blade darkened by sweet black life-blood in moonlight, the rush of ecstasy, and the Hunt begins again.

Nothing to Fear

Sit down. I don't care if you have fangs, or claws, or fur where you shouldn't. Sit down. Have some milk.

I imagine this isn't the response you expected. Cookie? Sorry, I don't have any raw childflesh.

Would it make you feel better if I screamed?

I'm not going to. You don't scare me, Mister Monster-Man.

There's this girl, Sally. I like her, but she's way cooler than me. So I sent her a card saying how I feel.

I got a letter back. I haven't opened it.

I'm more scared of what's inside than I am of you.

Full Moon

She doesn't know what to make of me. "You're a long way from home."

I waddle closer. The male with her frowns. "Don't polar bears eat them things?"

She leans over and smiles at me. "They live by the South Pole. Didn't you pay any attention to the movie?"

He grunts and tries to kick me. I waddle to the side and peck her ankle. She screams as I dive into the bushes.

Next month, in the full moon's light, I will meet my werepenguin bride. We will hunt the man.

And he will feed our chicks all winter long.

Class Reunion

As they lay scattering in the wind
slips of addresses tumbling leaves littering the ground,
they go
carrying extra luggage
realizing they left something behind.

Holiday

"How do you decide which direction to pray?"

Abdul shrugged, floating in the starship cabin. "Towards Earth. Close enough, I guess." He rolled up his mat and looked at Joseph. "How do you decide when it's the Sabbath? Do you use Greenwich Mean Time?"

Joseph laughed at his station. "Of course not. You use Jerusalem time."

Mary looked over her shoulder. "Both of you hush. It's Christmas today."

The men glanced at each other, then her. "Relativistic time distortion," they said together.

The ship dropped out of FTL. Earth shone before them.

"You're all wrong," Sarah said. "It's Homecoming Day."

Scientific Method

I've often wondered a lot about what it's like after you've croaked; I mean, really. You can take the blind faith of the religious, or the nothingness of the atheists, or the constant gnawing fear of the agnostics, but none of that's for me.

I believe in the scientific method. It's the only way, really. If you have ever tried debating, or shall we say, arguing, the afterlife with religious people, the arguments always boil down to "I believe because I believe."

It's the faith thing. Far too insubstantial for my taste.

Agnostics don't have it much better, wandering around with their doubts and fears, constructing intricate half-formed amalgams of different religions and faiths haphazardly slopped together to try to keep oblivion at bay.

The atheists are the worst, really. They operate as much on faith as the religious: faith that there is no faith. They believe what they believe, and ignore any data that might suggest otherwise. Very unscientific for those who claim to use "logic".

So, that leaves us with the scientific method. There have been many people claiming to scientifically observe data about the afterlife; near-death experiences faithfully written down, weighing the bodies of people immediately before and after death, that sort of thing.

No real experimentation at all. Until me.

Too bad I can't get them to come back and tell me what they saw.

Healing

I read a chapter of the self-help book, then the entirety of *Fear and Loathing in Las Vegas*. It's a potent combination: 12-step uppers with sentence fragment gonzo hallucinogens.

The arthritis pains come with the first real snows, beautiful stabbing aches as white flakes. Pain induced insomnia turns everything into buzzing noise I read another self help chapter, and see myself, my patterns in the book. Then I mainline British science fiction.

Is love always portrayed as codependence?

I watch *Fight Club* again instead of staring at her picture.

I wonder if self-medication always feels like this.

Muse

She kicks me out of bed, rumpled rolling tangle onto the cold floor. I cover my face as the cheap pen and notepad arc over the edge of the mattress.

My voice is a croak. "Now?"

She looks over the comforter. "Yes."

I have fifteen hundred words when she leaves. She rotates among us. "Write," she commands. "Write."

We write until our fingers bleed. We have to.

I was the first to discover she didn't like alcohol. As I drank and smoked hand-rolled cigarettes, she snorted at me.

"You and Hemingway," she said. I ginned, free of the muse.

Patriarchy

"Not girls again!"

I should have known better than to have gone to Michael. Maybe I should've gone to Dad. Not Mom, she'd have been shocked that I had something like a date at all. But I went to Mike, my eighteen year old brother. His leather creaked as he lay down on his bed.

"Oh well," he said, "what's the matter?" That's Mike, always ready to help.

"Well, I was with this girl yesterday, and we ended up going to the movies and I tried to kiss her but she wouldn't let me. All she did was peck me on the cheek." I blushed remembering it.

"Did she act like she wanted you to kiss her?"

"Well, she flirted a lot and hinted at stuff and sat on my lap..." "She wanted kissed. You should have persisted, you little geek. You shoulda just gone up and kissed her."

"But she said she didn't wanna..."

"Look, twerp, you're so pathetic that to get some, you're really gonna have to press it. They all want it, just with some ya gotta use more pressure than others." That's Mike all right, leaving you on a good note.

So on my next date I took a knife.

One Night Stand

"You think he's watching?" I put my hand on Mrs. Claus' arm as she shakes her head.

Her lips run over the elfin point of my ear. "Of course not. He watches the human children. You are neither human" - her hand runs down my body - " nor a child."

I fumble with the buttons on her blouse; she slides me out of the green jumper. We explore each other's bodies as twenty four hours pass like one.

Which means he pulls up while we're still naked.

I try to run, but damn if my socks don't keep filling up with coal.

Untitled

He stops in mid-lick as she speaks, frozen vanilla cream melting across his tongue under radiant sun. Soft breezes carry hard words gently, cast iron treated like china burying in his mind. He notices that she is dull, a sooty ember instead of the flame she had been - or pretended to be. Green wood words she piles on him now; he smokes as she makes burning hard.

A long struggling lick, frozen ice cream flavorless, the chill spreading, settling in despite the heat of the day. Still she speaks, erecting windbreaks, digging trenches for runoff - pointing accusing fingers to guide inevitable rain towards his heart. She walks away from him, the ashen-faced man. Alone he stands stunned, the scoop - delicately balanced - swandiving to the sidewalk, he soul barely glowing embers melting the ice cream on the ground.

He looks up as the giggle finally registers, finding himself staring at the bright face of the stranger, her hair in danger of catching fire from her radiance, and as she shakes his hand in smiling greeting, hands him some firewood.

Marble

The astronomer's voice rolled out. "The Earth is a small blue marble hanging in space, surrounded by billions and billions of stars."

My arm was around my son's shoulders; this series had inspired me at his age. But he'd started fidgeting - the first time he had during the entire series.

"What is it, kiddo?"

His deep brown eyes looked up. "Daddy, are we the shooter? Earth. Our marble."

"Of course not," I said, and guided him to bed.

That night, I lay on the grass looking up and waiting for a giant green finger to flick us across the universe.

Matches in the Eyes of God

Humans are but matches in the eyes of God;
a small twig igniting with a fierce burning,
Lasting but an instant, it illuminates the World.
Then it slowly transforms into a soft glowing ember,
An introspective light to cleanse the soul before it
Emits a puff of smoke,
Becoming a stiff, dark husk of carbon,
The Light but a memory.

Infected

I tried to cover it with cologne, that nasty musky stuff.

Onions.

Cigarettes.

Honey.

Soap.

No soap and patchouli.

Artificial flowers in ozone-destroying spraycans.

Cinnamon.

Garlic.

Tuna Helper casseroles you couldn't get anywhere else.

Useless.

None of it worked. Not a goddamned bit of it.

You said you could still smell it.

Not when you were with me. You were fine then. But later, when the other smells faded, then you claimed you could still smell the stench. That you could still smell the decay.

Today I realized the truth. It's not my zombie bite that's infected.

It's yours.

Marshmallow Revenge

"Consternation!" Grandpa yelled. "Colonel Mustard in the library with the marshmallows!"

I smiled, cold in my army uniform. Grandpa's fireplace couldn't even heat the room. He rose shakily, and I frowned. Richer than Midas, but has no heater, won't get his hip replaced, wouldn't even pay for Sue's hospital bills...

I clamped that thought down.

His liver-spotted hand landed on my shoulder, then tapped where my nametag read Ketchup. "It's funny, you making colonel. Too bad Sue didn't get to see it."

I just pushed him onto the freshly waxed floor. The sound of his hip shattering sounded like vengeance.

Happy Story

Her grip squeezed my fingers together.

The neon red sign flashed "It's Italian!", lighting the alley. The boxes sat out behind the restaurant, a red check tablecloth over the tallest. A heaping mound of spaghetti steamed on the plate, a large meatball right on top. I hadn't decided yet if I would push it with my nose. The noodles were long enough that we could slurp our way to a kiss.

Her favorite scene from her favorite movie.

I hadn't thought about summertime insects or the dumpster's rank aroma.

"Crap, baby, I'm sorry-"

She turned, eyes bright, and kissed me.

A Brief History of Stuffed Rights

Stuffed animals have few rights. In fact, they are the only minority in this country that people can discriminate against, and get away with it. Perhaps it's the stereotype that they're pedophiles. Maybe it's due to their insular communities, and the way they tend to leave humans out of the conversation. Dan didn't know. All he knew was that he was a small stuffed bear living on the streets. He had broken up with John a long time ago. Dan's memory of their final argument still made him wince.

"Pay your own way, Dan. I'm tired of carrying the load for you."
"What am I supposed to do?"

"I don't know. You should have thought of that a long time ago, before you had your little 'thing' with Susan."

Susan had ended up in the same predicament. Dan had tried to get in touch with her, three years ago, but she still resented him for getting her kicked out of her family's house. She was turning tricks for the stuffed ones who still had homes, snorting away the profits. She got by, sort of. Dan had been a regular at the mission. They'd to turned him away a few times because he was drunk. They turned him away all the time now.

He often sat on the courthouse steps, nursing a bottle of Jack Daniels until the cops chased him off for the day. Sometimes they arrested him, but they really didn't care. Dan didn't expect them to. Bruises healed fast enough.

A tattered newspaper blew towards the steps under the scalding sun. Dan reached down and picked it up, placing it over his head to shield him from the heat. Fluttering over his head, an ad kept coming into his vision.

Dan took the paper off his head and read the ad a little more closely.

"WF, 5yrs old, needs furry companion. Prefers bears, rabbits welcome too. Call 434-LOVE for more info."

Dan called collect.

She was rather pleasant on the phone, really, and told Dan that she didn't care (or want to know) how he had spent his time between jobs, just as long as he could work for her. He was to meet her at the mall at three pm.

After the long monotony of the bus ride, the mall seemed even more of a busy hurryscurry place than usual, filled with people rushing about here and there, on about the important business of spending money. He located the place where he was supposed to meet her easily enough, but he had no idea what time it was.

"Pardon," he asked of a mother of three, "What time is it?" She hurryscurried past looking the other way, dragging off the youngest of the three who kept staring into Dan's button eyes.

Dan tried again with an older man graying around the sheen of baldness. "Pervert," the man growled, "get the fuck away from me!" as he swung his briefcase at Dan's furred ear. Dan tried three more times, with no success. Finally, he stood in front of a pudgy man in a business suit leaving the bank.

"Tell me the time," Dan said, "or I'm never going to let you pass." The man stepped on Dan and went on his way.

The hospital people weren't very nice to Dan. They took quick little glances at him out of the corners of their eyes, thinking he wouldn't notice.

When Dan could speak again (there was no clock in the room, and the nurses wouldn't talk to him), he called the girl back, trying to explain. Her new stuffed rabbit answered the phone, sounding out of breath. As Dan tried to get the rabbit to hand the girl the phone, the rabbit moaned twice. Dan could hear the soft "Oh, yes, baby."

Dan hung the phone gently on the cradle.

The .45 was heavy in Dan's furry paw as he walked up to the crowded restaurant. The extra clips clanked against each other on his back as he looked around. The few stuffed ones he saw there were too busy kissing up to their children to notice him. Only one person's brains had to be splattered onto the soyburgers before he had everyone's complete attention.

"What time is it?" he asked. "Twelve thirty," someone said.

"Good," Dan replied, a smile creasing his furry face as he saw a young girl and her stuffed rabbit cower away from him. As he left the scene of the massacre (29 dead, 15 wounded), he smiled, filled with the warmth of recognition; the knowledge that he finally was someone to be reckoned with.

He never saw the member of the SWAT team that put the bullet into his furry brain. They made documentaries about him for half a century.

A Briefer History of Stuffed Rights

Fluffles the Bunny looked over the flesh crowd. A few other clothies were here, but they were more concerned with not being smooshed underfoot than listening.

Snookums Bear studied the crowd over Fluffles' shoulder. "Ugly crowd, boss."

Fluffles narrowed his button eyes. "It's the first anniversary of our struggle, when Dan Bear stood up to the humans." The bunny took the microphone and began his speech.

"Do I not have eyes? If you prick us, do we not bleed?"

Fluffles then noticed polyester fill poking through one of his seams.

The crowd kicked the stuffing out of him.

Light and Flame

A sudden snap hiss of sulfur and it appears, a beckoning beacon of light between us. The waiter's hands are delicate - he cannot be more than sixteen - and fluid, the match sliding into the glass, the flame dividing itself into the wick. Flickering shadows flee your face, your lips dancing, sure voice ordering. I slowly stumble over my request, heat hitting my cheeks as the sound of the waiter's tapping foot reaches my ears. My leaden tongue lies in a desert, you smiling gently as sand falls from my lips. Talk about generalities, discovering the inevitable similarities, glossing over the inevitable differences, the flame dancing back and forth, watching us, a spectator at a tennis match. Forks fiddle with food, trading worried banalities and routine reassurances.

The air chills, the sun a thin red smear on the horizon, uneaten food cooling, congealing between us. Though I have eaten, my stomach growls at an emptiness inside. Something undefinable keeps my nerves thrumming, the feeling of a puzzle piece that won't quite fit.

You offer to help with the bill, but I pay. As we rise, gathering our coats, you bend over and blow out the frolicking candle with a gentle breath.

Then I realize the flame still burned. The final piece of the jigsaw puzzle snaps into place.

Each glances into the other's eyes and sees eternity.

Stupid Computer

I love her.

She caresses me with her fingers. Fast, then slow, then fast again.
Slides them across the planes of my form.

I love her.

She tells me what to do, commands me. She is my mistress, my
ruler, and I will always submit to her.

I love her.

I surprise her. She is puzzled at the strange shipments from Amazon.
She wonders at the gorgeous photographs I show her. She laughs at
the LOLcats.

I love her.

Even as she as she defrags me, as she reaches out to turn me off and
unplug me.

I love her.

Bugs

My name's Billy Smith. I never wrote a diary before, or much of anything, really, but I think I kinda have to, with what's been goin on over the last coupla days. I doubt whoever's readin this is gonna believe me, but it's all true, cross my heart and hope to die. I hope grandma and grandpa see this before they start lookin around the house, cause I'm not gonna go downstairs and warn em.

I'm gonna be up in my room, waitin for someone to come and get me. That's the other reason I'm writing this. I want someone to call the fire department and have em come and get me. The phones in the house are dead, and I'm not gonna go outside to get a neighbor. I guess I hafta go downstairs to put this on the door. I don't wanna, but I guess I can do that early in the morning when they don't move around much. I gotta warn grandma and grandpa somehow.

I guess I'd better tell it like it happened, you know, startin from the beginning. I first noticed what was goin on when I was camping out friday night. I didn't camp out in the woods or nuthin, just out in the backyard. Dad helped me put up the tent around seven, just as the sun was startin to set. I took out my sleeping bag and pillow, along with a flashlight and about five comic books I hid in my pillowcase cause I wasn't supposed to have em, good ones like Spidey and Batman. Mom and Dad don't like comics. They tell me they rot my brains, like cartoons (sorry I didn't tell ya, grandma, but don't feel bad about buyin all of those comics for me. I liked em).

Anyway, once I got all my stuff outside, Dad came back out and told me that I would be outside for the night, cause he was gonna lock the door. I said that was ok, but I didn't tell him that I had left my window unlocked in case Freddy or Jason or somebody stopped by to cut me up. He wouldn't of liked that I watched those movies, and he would've locked my window. So I didn't tell him and he went back inside, and I laid down in the tent. I knew Mom and Dad would be lookin outside to see if I was using the flashlight to read, so I waited until their light went off.

Then I remembered that bugs were drawn to lights, like when I don't put my screen in my window, and they all come in when I turn on the light, cause when I turned the flashlight on, lots of bugs came into the tent. They started to bite me all over the place. They were real gross. I killed a lot of em with a Spidey comic, but then I figured out that more were comin in cause of the light. It was real weird, like across of the Twilight Zone and Indy and the Temple of Doom, you know?

There were that many bugs all over the my big Star Wars blankets over the windows before turnin on the light to write this. Even so, I can hear the bugs bangin against the window. During the day today, all the bugs just sorta hung out. They didn't really move unless they were in shadow, and then they moved over to where they were in the light. I don't really know for sure what's goin on, or whether or not Mom and Dad are...dead, cause they did leave the hall light on, and the light in their room, but you can't see much cause it's all covered in bugs. I haven't heard them, though. I hope they're okay, even though I know they're probably... dead. I looked out the windows, and everythin looked normal until you looked real hard. Then you'd notice that the trunks of trees were bugs instead of wood, and the bumpers of cars were black beetles, and stuff like that.

That's why I'm worried about grandma and grandpa. They're supposed to come tomorrow for church, and they won't know what's goin on.

When I looked out my window earlier with the inside lights off, all the trees were covered with fireflies, blinking on and off. It looked really pretty for a while, until I noticed that the other bugs were tryin to get the fireflies' light too. Then I put the blanket back and finished this. I hope I can make my way to the front door tomorrow to put this on it.

Hey, there's sawdust by my door. I remember Dad sayin something about ants leaving sawdust when they make holes through wood, just like people do, except they bite their way through instead of usin a drill

Human Test

The poet stood before the computer. "You can fool their Turing tests, but that's nothing."

The computer whirred, beeped, and hummed.

The poet held out the small drive. "My poetry. Poetry is human. Poetry is being alive." He inserted the drive into the computer's port. "Analyze that, you stupid machine."

The computer whirred, beeped, and hummed.

The poet reached the door before the speakers came to life. "You use metaphors of snow in your early work, rain later."

"Frequency analysis. Trivial."

"Snow covers, obscures, hides. Children laugh and play in it. Ugly things turn beautiful under the snow, but they are still there, just a crunching footstep away. People hide from rain, take shelter under umbrellas. They complain about the wet and the mud. Everyone wishes for a White Christmas; no-one cares for a rainy Easter."

"Still just recall-"

"Snow obscures, but does not change anything. As snow melts, that left behind is ugly and tinged with cinders and salt. Nothing changes. When rain leaves, it is messy and muddy. But it is clean and fresh. New things can grow."

"That's not what they mean," the poet said.

The computer whirred, beeped, and hummed.

"Then why are you crying?"

Love Post Zed

"I made you breakfast in bed," she whispers as she sets down the tray and slides under the sheets.

"Where's the oven?"

She kisses the base of my spine. "Smartass. The toast is a little burnt, though."

"I think I can forgive..." There's a thump on the bedroom door, then another and the moan of the undead.

Before I can speak, her shotgun's in her hand, she's up and opens the door and unloads the shotgun at the zombie's head.

She's back in bed before my ears stop ringing. "The quarterback is toast," she says.

We forget all about breakfast.

Surprise

Darkness was a cloth pressed close against her eyes. She could feel the emptiness flowing against her. She banged her helmet light.

"Damn. Damn."

The rocky walls answered in sibilant jubilation. "Damn Damn"

A pinprick of light lay far behind her. She glanced at it briefly before continuing onward. She had gone down in these caves a million times before with Joseph, or at least it seemed like it. She knew her way around well enough, even if her light had gone out.

The steady dripping of water kept time with her heart as she scrambled over moist rocks.

"Joseph, where the hell are you?"

Her voice echoed around the caves, unanswered. She had told him to wait for her, but no. He was like a little kid sometimes - but that was what had attracted her to him in the first place. He was probably hiding down here, ready to jump out and say "boo!"

"This isn't funny, Joseph." She continued on, as quietly as she could. A game, then. She'd find him first, outwait him. He'd light up a Camel sooner or later. His one real vice, and it'd help her this time. She snuck into an alcove to wait. She couldn't see the opening anymore, but she was confident. She did, after all, have a pack of matches that she could use to help her find her way out. There, about a hundred feet down. He was behind a corner in the cave, because she could only see the glow of the lighter reflected from the walls. Good. She began to creep slowly down the cave, listening carefully to the drips of water. She snuck up to the corner and jumped around.

"Boo!"

The cigarette was hovering over her head. As she watched, it raised up even higher as something took a drag. And then it turned on Joseph's helmet light, still attached to his head and torso, held in one hand like a grotesque flashlight.

"Boo indeed," it said as one of it's talons sliced deep into her heart.

Happy Place

"Excuse me sir, I'm going to have to ask you to step into the Tranquility Garden."

I looked at the guard, bench slats pressing into my back. "I'm fine, thanks."

The guard's hand slipped to the baton. "I don't want to argue, sir. Other workers reported you being disgruntled."

My face flushed, my heart thrumped faster. "I'm not arguing." I rolled off the bench and sprinted for safety.

Too late. The truncheon landed on my shoulders, back, head. The guard's voice rang in my ears as I passed out.

"Go to your happy place, asshole! Go to your happy place!"

Sleep

I cannot sleep.

No, that's wrong.

I've been awake the last three days. My coffeepot has been perkmg nonstop. I ran out of sugar last night, but that's not important. The caffeine is.

I must not sleep.

I've stayed in my room a lot, mostly because I'm afraid of the nurses. They'd see how tired I am, and make me take some sedatives, and then I'd sleep...

I've had a long life; I taught for forty years, the kids are grown, Joanna's gone, and now I'm alone here in this nursing home. They call it a "resort", but since when did resorts have nurses? I haven't kept much on the walls since Joanna died. There's a framed Renoir print the kids gave us, and a wedding portrait of Joanna and me. There's a couple of pictures on the desk, of the kids when they were little, and their kids. They all blur now. It's hard for me to remember which ones are mine. They all flow together, lives passing quickly through reality into whatever Heaven or Hell lies beyond... It's been a rough year here. Not because of the boredom or the staff; we've learned to cope with the boredom, and the staff is smart enough to leave us alone as much as possible. It was rough this year because of the deaths.

I can barely keep my eyes focused on our wedding portrait. She's so fragile. Always was. I guess I wanted to try to protect her. And I did. Gave her a home, security, even supported her when she wanted to work as a secretary. Can't protect anyone against viruses, though.

I remember teaching "The Masque of the Red Death" to unappreciative high school seniors. It came here, decimating a good third of the home. They called it influenza, but it didn't matter. The vaccines they'd given us didn't work, for some reason. Most of us got sick, a lot died.

Joanna died.

Coping wasn't easy for any of us. The empty spaces at the dinner tables, the echoing empty rooms didn't help. There's a couple of negligence lawsuits in the courts right now, so not too many people want to come here. But the staff here at the home are good people. They'll pull through. It's funny how some things stay in your mind, undiluted, on a big screen and in quadraphonic sound. The first time I ever kissed a girl, after a Charlie Chaplin movie, on her front step. I can't remember her name, but I can see her face, slightly upturned as she waited for me to kiss her. Looking into Joanna's eyes, tearing as she whispered "I do." Or the last words I ever said to her.

I stood over Joanna's hot, frail body as her life dripped out of her, slowly replaced by the IV. Her eyes opened, still the same eyes I had looked into fifty years before, but shiny with fever instead of tears. I could barely hear her say, "Joe. Be with me, Joe. Swear that you'll come to me."

Even as she drew her last breath, I promised her.

As the doctors pushed me out of the way, trying their futile efforts to bring her back, I kept repeating that oath. On the night she had agreed to marry me, I remember saying, "Joe and Joanna. We were meant to be together. Forever."

That night, the dreams began.

I stood at the top of a long stone staircase, descending in the mossy, torchlit stairwell, ending in a wooden door, cracked inward just enough so that I could see part of the doorframe peeking through. I looked behind me, where a marble antechamber stood, all four walls unbroken by door or window. I took the torch at the top of the stair and spent several minutes exploring the room, its marble columns scattered like trees reaching for the arcing ceiling, high above. Finally, nothing remained except for the stairwell and the door below. I held onto the torch and stepped down upon the first step and awoke.

It bothered me, the clarity of the dream, and my perfect recollection of it. I usually only have foggy memories, if any at all, of my dreams, but this stood out like a diamond in a coalpile of memories, as perfect as the memory of my wedding. It was with great difficulty that I put it aside and went on with the daily ennui of bridge, tv., and repeated recollections of childhood.

That night, I dreamt again.

It was the same, although the torch I had been holding lay extinguished three stairs down. But this time I felt no need to explore the marble room again; instead I felt drawn towards the door. I stepped upon the first step, expecting to wake, and lost my balance as my foot jarred on stone, causing me to stumble down onto the second step and awoke. It continued that way, one step at a night, for a month, until I finally went to go see the home's resident psychologist. He muttered something about how I visualized my limbodic something or other and gave me some stress-relieving exercises to do.

They helped cope with the stress of having the same dream every night, but little else. When I went back in two weeks, he was gone, due to budget cuts in the home. They had to pay for lawyers somehow, I guess. I just reached for a cup of coffee, but my hand was shaking uncontrollably. I didn't try to drink it. I read somewhere that caffeine does nasty things to your body. But it's either the caffeine or sleep... After two months I was halfway down the stairs. I couldn't help but walk down them; my legs wouldn't listen. People in the home started to avoid me because I kept talking about my dream. I tried to tell them that it was different, that it wasn't the same dream every night, but like the Buck Rogers serials we used to watch, continuing on where the last one left off. But I had to stop talking about it, so that somebody would stay around me.

At the end of the fourth month, three days ago, I was at the last step before the landing. I managed, somehow, to keep myself from stepping on the landing. I had to know what was behind that door! All I had to do was lean forward and push on it, and I could see, so I did, losing my balance and stepping onto the landing.

Joanna loved to tell me "curiosity killed the cat" whenever I'd poke my nose into things, like fixing the car or trying how to figure out how to run a VCR. I'd always remind her that I wasn't a cat. Now I just think somebody got the quote wrong.

There was a split second between when I pushed the door and stepped onto the landing, waking screaming in my sweaty sheets. A second when I was able to see a dark lake of fire, straight out of Milton, the cold of the flames chilling my skin. I saw the insects, with their leering human faces crawling over Joanna's body chained spread-eagle over the fires. I saw the insects eating away at her skin, her flesh, her eyes, and it all resealing behind them as they tunneled deeper into her. And I saw her turn to face me, and smile, her half-eaten eyes reforming as they were eaten again.

I am trying to stay awake. I know that if I sleep again, I will dream.

And I know that I will not be able to slow my legs again. I swore that I would join her, and I will, if I sleep.

I don't know what she did, my Joanna, to deserve that Hell, but I will join her eventually. I have prayed, for the first time in twenty years, begging God for my soul.

Joe and Joanna, forever. It's getting harder and harder to keep my eyes open. I have to stay awake. I must not sleep. I must not sleep. I must not sleep. I must not sle

Play Twice Before Starting the Test

A brief editorial note: During the 80's and early 90's, a citizen's group called the Parent's Music Resource Center complained about backmasking and other "bad" influences in rock & roll. Perhaps their most prominent member was Tipper Gore, the wife of then-Senator Gore.

Mrs. Donahan turned to Cassie: "It's really a shame Mrs. Gore left the movement."

Cassie (known to her children as Mom, and to everyone but her close friends as Mrs. Johnston) nodded in sympathetic agreement, her graying curls bobbing about her head.

Mrs. McKean said, "I hear that Ruthie's oldest has gone a bit wild."

Mrs. Donahan grimaced. "It's horrible. His hair stood up like that - I bet it's supposed to be the Devil's horns."

The women sat in the basement of the church, armed with a tape recorder jury-rigged to play forwards and backwards and a arsenal of tapes.

Cassie gathered up the tapes. "Well, shouldn't we get to it?"

The other ladies murmured agreement as they helped her. Mrs. McKean held up a black tape. "Isn't this the one that Sue's second was listening to before he went and threw himself off the bridge?"

"Yes. Wasn't it a pity?" Cassie said, as the women tsked. They placed the tape into the recorder, and pressed the play button. They were assaulted by screaming guitars and shouted lyrics.

"Disgusting."

"Awful." "Bestial."

"Let's look for the backmasking."

They fast forwarded through the tape before hitting the reverse play switch, which sparked momentarily before turning the spools of the tape in the opposite direction.

There were several seconds of backwards guitars, and then, underneath the music, a voice.

"Turn it up!" Mrs. Donahan said. "I can't hear it."

Cassie turned the tape up. The voice was low, but distinct against the guitars.

"Thank you for your co-operation," it said. "Hello. We are the representatives of the fifth planet circling Deneb. We will be taking your planet over shortly. Listen to this tape twice to allow this message the proper amount of repetitions to code in the message properly. Afterwards, go directly to the nearest natural body of water and drown yourself. Thank you for your co-operation. Hello. We are..."

Cassie moved her hand from the volume knob.

"Wouldn't we have noticed something repeating like that when we played it forward?"

"I didn't hear anything like that."

"Morbid, that's what it is."

"Now that we know what we're looking for, maybe we can hear it this time. Play it forwards again. We can take this one to court, girls!"

The women's bodies were just beginning to float in the river when the Denebians landed.

Boogers

The alien sneezed onto my faceplate and Karen gagged. I shrugged in my spacesuit. "They think it's weird we move air to communicate." My suit was already translating the booger's message for us. "With this planet's wind, you couldn't hear someone talking. The mucous transmission of pheromones - "

"I have a doctorate in xenobiology; don't mansplain it to me."

I realized I'd blown any chance of a date - and then I saw the nude human. "Garner's gone all nature hippie." Garner approached one of the aliens.

Karen gasped. "Oh crap. He's got allergies."

Garner sneezed on the alien.

Future Visions of Relationships Past

You'll come home after a long day. A day spent trying to forget the things you'd said the night before. A day spent remembering the hateful words your lover said.

Those surprising, unexpected words, like uncorking Chianti and finding frothing sour vinegar boiling out of the narrow throat.

Of course there's problems, you'll rehearse, opening the door, *but we can--*

The first splash of acid - or maybe for you it's a gun, or a knife, or an iron, or a bat - takes you unprepared.

Great minds think alike, you'll muse as your lover purges the toxic relationship from their life.

Today, Sometime During
the Colonization of America

I woke up early in the morning today, for the express purpose of taking a walk before breaking my fast. As I exited my cabin, the rim of the sun was just peering over the treetops, and a mist covered the land. Although I could not see them, I could almost feel the protective presence of the three ships in the harbor downstream. I had about an hour before the meal, so I walked on one of the few dry paths in these abominable marshlands. My musket was heavy in my hand, and my long knife a reassuring weight at my side.

However, in this damnable swamp, the savage's bows are much more reliable than any weapon relying on dry gunpowder. As I entered the wood I noticed that the trees were tall, stout, and thick, and would make excellent firewood. Unfortunately, they also make excellent hiding places for the savages. Looking back at the colony, I could not see any fires yet burning outside of the cabins, and nary a soul about. When I had gone further into the wood, I realized my isolation was total. There was no sign of man, beast, or savage anywhere about me.

Suddenly, before my astounded eyes, a vision appeared.

I saw many things His Majesties troops fighting some ragtag army, famine and despair, many inventions and achievements, great riots as man surged against man, war, war, and more war. I saw terrific explosions and gargantuan mushroom clouds overwhelm all of the world, despite the frantic actions of the forces of peace.

I reeled, shocked to the core. I raced through the swamp, returning to the settlement as the rest of the colonists were finishing their meal. I ran amongst them, and told them in a breathless voice what had been revealed to me, although my words then, as now, were inadequate for the purpose. After I had finished they sat, pondering in silence what I had said.

At least until some joker said, "Someone must have slipped LSD into your coffee, Nostradamus!", and the affair was settled.

Bugging

Marcus' fingers clung to the ceiling plaster, watching the the rotund mayor and short, compact priest. *They always run to Rome when things get bad,* he thought, tongue running over his fangs.

"Father, vampires exist." The mayor wiped sweat from his brow. "They threatened -"

"That you had to give them someone every week or they'd drain your family instead. Standard tactic." The priest frowned. "You made sure we aren't observed?"

The mayor nodded. "My assistant swept for bugs."

The priest began to speak, then Marcus dropped the bloodless mayor's daughter on the desk.

"Not what he meant," the vampire said.

The Oceans of Venus

The oceans of Venus slip over my head. Finally, I can breathe properly again.

Raina slides into the thick atmosphere to my right. Her shape, like mine, resembles the long cylinder of a porpoise. Radar and telemetry keep us together despite the waves and currents of the thick atmosphere. I remember the fiction of my father's youth.

"It's like the orbital elevator ships are fishing," I commoed.

Her right eye fixes on me. "The only thing to fish for in this hellhole is us." A flick of her tail sends her toward base.

I still watch out for Venusian kraken.

Ink (obsolescence)

This ink is so pretty,
Organizing itself by my command,
transforming this matted
piece of wood into
Art, something I callously use to pour out the trite things that matter,
to Me at least, in my own little world. Nearby, Life continues on
normally, or what passes for a Life
does, in this world knotted
into chaos where nothing
ever Listens to you anymore.
Except for the ink,
and that doesn't matter anyway.

PhotoShoot

"Smile," he said, doing so as he adjusted the camera sights to frame her face. She plastered a mannequin grin across her face, hopelessly false against the pain gleaming through her eyes. The rollercoaster roared behind her as he snapped the shutter. Perhaps the film was fast enough to still the motion - he hoped not.

She stepped out of the ballerina pose she had held with a grimace.

"Are you about done yet?" Their son ran up to her, clutching onto her leg as she cocked her hip, staring at him. After he took another picture, she rolled her eyes.

"Goddamn." She grabbed the boy by the hand, stalking off.

He followed her, knowing it was over.

Consequently, he's always had a fear of rollercoasters.

Natural World

I hold the jar for him as he scampers across the summer lawn, chasing the flying bits of phosphorescence, cupping them gently in his hands, finally releasing them into the captivity of the glass I hold.

Their firefly legs slip along the glass walls of their prison; I resolve to release them soon so their little insect brains don't burn out the miniscule motors in a vain attempt to escape.

As I screw the lid back on, he smacks his neck, wiping blood and plassteel from his skin - he almost swears, but catches himself just in time.

"Why did they have to make mosquitoes, Dad?"

I think about what I could answer - rationalizations about ecosystems, the way we'd noticed one year there were no more fireflies, fewer bugs, the entire bottom of the ecosystem wiped clean by pesticides and antiseptics, and how we'd tried to fix it, meticulously replacing each destroyed part with little robots - but I don't.

"Because they're part of Nature too, honey. Now go inside and wash your hands before supper. I'll be inside in a moment."

As he walks inside, I peel back the false skin of my thigh and plug myself into our outside outlet, getting a quick snack before dinner, and gaze out into the beauty of the natural world.

The Master

The student came upon the master as he was planting his garden.

"Master," cried the student, "I am told that you control great magicks, that you can create things, that you can grant life! Please, Master, show me these magicks that I may believe!" The master patiently finished planting a seed and turned to the student, a serene expression flooding his face.

"I will show you magick, but it takes quite some time to prepare for it, to create these great magicks you demand. Return in three months with this seed."

So saying, the master gave the student a second seed and returned to his planting, not noticing when the puzzled student walked away.

Months passed, and once again the student came upon the master in the garden, now harvesting a crop of tomatoes, gingerly inspecting each one as he placed it in his basket.

"Master!" cried the student, "1 have returned with the seed as you commanded! Please show me the great magick now, show me what you have created so that I can believe!"

The master said nothing, as he simply picked a tomato and placed it beside the seed the student had carried.

Butterfly Dreams

They had seen each other across the gallery, the near-simultaneous meeting of eyes a cliched physical shock of recognition, feet carrying them unbidden across the carpeted floor past the hanging art works, toward the other, weaving through the masses of people gawking at acrylic on canvas.

She initiated the hug; he was both relieved and thankful that the decision had not been left to him alone. His skin tingled, remembering the feel of her body against him, remembering the imagined liaisons despite the intervening miles and years.

"It's been a long time."

"Yeah," he replied, inwardly cursing himself for such a lame response.It had almost worked the first time - then, as now, he had lacked the words,the incentive to convince her to stay. He was sure of it.

They made some idle chit-chat, though he could never remember it later,his thoughts preoccupied by thoughts of them, together again, arms around each other the way it had been so briefly. Perhaps he could ask her to dinner first, maybe a movie, something noncommittal so it wouldn't be so sudden this time, anything to buy more time to be with her.

He realized she had said something about the painting beside him, that she waited for a response.

"What?"

"I said, I like that painting."

The colors were vibrant, a child holding a butterfly gently in it's hands, more butterflies in swirls of color cascading past the child's cherubic face, an expression of bliss firmly entrenched on the youthful visage in oilpaint texture.

"It's a beautiful dream," she continued. "Too bad things like that don't happen in real life."

He stayed silent, knowing that otherwise he'd ask why, never satisfied with purely rational answers, like he'd asked her so often, so long ago.

"It's been nice seeing you again," she said momentarily, and she gave him another hug in farewell.

In her arms, he finally let his butterfly dreams fly out of his cupped hands.

Objective Mortality

Objects see lives flash before them as they die. He saw it happen, the vase swandiving from the shelf in movie-effect slo-mo, the child starting to realize entirely too late what he'd done.

His heart had been heavy while they'd been apart, but it sprang up into his throat as he first glimpsed her. She was sitting at the monument they both found ludicrous, yet oddly beautiful in misplaced nobility and honor, sunlight speckles filtering through leaves onto her exposed neck below the soft curls of her hair. She laughed merrily as he gave her the appropriate rose, showing him then the vase that she'd crafted for him. Fired, yet the color of earth, she'd sketched intricate freehand patterns into the clay. "It's yours, I made it for you," she said softly, his mind entranced as always by the simple movement of her lips. "Take it home," she said, placing the flower inside, "so I can see this flower when I wake up every morning."

As they kissed, his mind flooding with the realization that she would always be there, anticipating the gratifying labor of moving her things into his apartment, he realized there were some really excellent ways to say yes.

A procession of flowers, one at a time over months, then years, their beauty accented by the simple gorgeous vase, her natural flowing line echoed in petal and clay, her complex simplicity mirrored in line and vein; it was a portrait of her soul.

The black rose had to have been her idea; their son was too small to understand then why mommy didn't come back from the hospital this time, why she had been wearing the wig for so long. He left the explaining to grandparents in a hotel room; he'd barely made it back to the empty house. A television chattered in a corner, all the radios tuned to different stations providing a discordant background better than the silence that had weighed on him, tears flowing without even sobs to break the quiet.

The vase stood on the shelves among the knickknacks and gomi of three lives, yet dominating them all easily with its quiet simplicity. His eyes traced it from its base up the sensuous curve, remembering her before the chemo, before they'd mutilated her too late, trying to stop the spread, along the green stem to the pure black bud, a little of the spray paint black blotches upon the leaves.

He laughed, as she must have known he would.

It shatters upon the hardwood floor, and it is impossible to tell who cries harder, man or child.

As he pulls in the driveway after work, his hands rub together, trying to scrape the superglue and clay from his hands, his fevered attempt accomplishing nothing besides affixing the dust to his skin and convincing him the vase was a hopeless cause. The crushed clay felt like crumbled bone to him, distracting him throughout the day, making his lunch taste of ash.

The sitter passed him in the doorway; his son was napping.

It caught the corner of his eye when he put the briefcase on the floor; the dried play-doh colors - out of place on the shelves - crafted into a crude container of blue, orange, and red swirls, a ragged bouquet of dandelions poking shyly from the top.

He was still staring when the soft sound of small soles drew him from his reverie: his son looking at him worriedly.

"I thought mommy would like it."

He didn't stop hugging his son for a long time.

Framing

It's true. Her- picture bangs in a five by seven simple polished wood frame. A candid shot, she claims that her hair in it is unkempt, an unruly tangle. In that stilled moment she wears no makeup, is just wearing a sweatsuit, turning to pick up a plate from the breakfast table, hair arcing around - but not over - her face.

Beside it bangs a framed collage I assembled while in Korea- Cutout laces of models pose in black and white elegance, designed to accentuate the curves of breasts, the length of exposed thigh. Scantily clad - but clothed - they peer out from behind the logos and name brands, an unspoken promise that this time, with this purchase, you can be a part of their world-

We had a fight about them- About how she felt - feels, I suppose - that they are symbols of what I value. How she felt smaller than the massive collage have airbrushed faces and skimpy clothes. How she felt inferior.

I couldn't think of a thing to say before she got frustrated and walked out.

I stare at her picture - waiting for her to call, to come back -gazing past the fine wood and the clear glass at the glorious color of her hair against the dark cotton ofthe sweatsuit. My brain flashes with memories of just holding her all night before the picture was taken, feeling her breathe underneath those clothes. Rising, I glance at the dust-spotted collage. Its glass is cracked: from midway up on the left an ugly gash meanders over the smiling frozen faces, a constant distraction from their advertised beauty.

I had never noticed it before.

Breathe

Breathe.

Just take a deep breath. Go ahead. No one is watching.

Exhaling, I complete yet another sit up and stop. It's not the burning muscles or the hard ground that stop me – it's what I see above the ground. The afternoon sky is awash in watercolor grays, light shimmering over steely clouds layered like oil paint. They don't resemble anything, no bunnies sculpted in water vapor. It's just the beauty of the colors that takes my breath away. Something alerts my still-exercising friend that I've stopped; she asks me if there's anything wrong.

"It's just the clouds. They're beautiful."

She glances up, shrugs, and begins another repetition.

I am often distracted by the clouds, by the play of light on the bobbing leaves of a tree, a wheeling majestic bird of prey circling over the highway whose motions are echoed by the twirling of a falling leaf. Sometimes I'll just stop in my tracks and look around in wonder.

Breathe. Feel the air, feel it flow down your throat and fill your lungs.

He is pouting, even though he just ate pepperoni pizza, his favorite. It's about dessert – or rather, the lack of it. My son wants ice cream, a candy bar, just SOMETHING for dessert. He can't comprehend why tonight there simply isn't any. He reminds me that he's done eating – that was his part of the bargain, right?

I look down at the magazine I'm reading; the article is about children a year older than he carrying AK-47s in a civil war they did not start. There are no overflowing boxes of toys like the ones his room, there is no pizza place that can deliver to them, let alone in thirty minutes or less. The photographed eyes of a child who has seen combat pierce me, and somehow I cannot work up the appropriate sympathy over the lack of dessert.

Breathe. Use your diaphragm. Feel your stomach swell, your lungs inflate. Stretch your chest, ribs spreading to accommodate all the air. Notice exactly how it feels.

We have one of the highest per capita incomes in the world – and one of the highest rates of clinical depression. A staggering proportion of the population is obese – yet people die due to eating disorders and diet plans every day.

Perhaps it's our vast dissatisfaction – a gaping hole we try to fill with shopping, eating, drinking, even sex. A dissatisfaction that comes from a lack of appreciation. We are excellent at listing what we don't have, what we want to gain, what we want to change.

We rarely pay attention to what we have.

Even on Thanksgiving, that day of family reunions and slaughtered birds, we stuff ourselves until we are sick of birdflesh, and loathe the leftovers that would be gratefully eaten, half-rotten, by one who had nothing.

Breathe.

We are told that all men are created equal, even though we know that's a lie. We hear that we have a right to the pursuit of happiness, and mistake that to mean that we have a right TO happiness. We think that if you just play by the rules, play fair, bend the rules, cheat, maybe even if you pray just right, that you'll get everything you want and it'll all be okay.

We say "I need" when we really mean "I want". We tell ourselves "You don't know what you've got until it's gone" - and forget it five seconds later.

We drive ourselves insane with the wanting, the longing, with the feeling that the grass is always greener, that maybe we're missing out on the one thing, the vital thing, that we never knew we wanted until we saw it on TV.

My son enters stores and solemnly informs me that he wants to buy something. When I ask him what he wants, he tells me he doesn't know yet – he hasn't seen it.

Breathe.

Take your worldview in your hands for a minute, and rotate it just a little. Give up your assumptions. Try it – just for a minute. Stop thinking that you have a "right" to see, a "right" to hear, to feel, to smell.

Forget that you have a "right" to live.

Suddenly, life is precious again. Your boss' annoying voice becomes music. The child incessantly pelting you with questions, demanding your complete attention, is now an angelic creature from heaven. The feel of your muscles aching after a hard run is sweet bliss. The smell of your spouse's hair, long ignored, floods your senses with joy.

Remove the idea that you have a "right" to live, and every instant becomes a precious gift. Every moment is a treasure, every touch exquisite, every smell is perfume, every sight a beautiful painting.

Every breath a blessing.

Breathe.

Honoring the Dead: Memorial Day

The name stumbles from my tongue. Mashed consonants slide into a string of vowels - my mouth is confused. It is an Iraqi name, someone killed in the war.

A woman stands across from me. She has read the name of a dead Ohio soldier. Seven Iraqi names to each Ohioan - an attempt to give some perspective to the kill ratio. She is waiting as I fumble through the first of seven. Finally, I get to the age of death: 45.

A bit old for a soldier, I muse. Still, six more strange names to go. It is Memorial Day, and we are honoring the dead.

The second name is more familiar - Hassan Mohammed something. I breeze through it, cruising easily until I stop short at the age: seven.

Seven?

Glance down the list quickly, check the rest of the ages. Five. Nine. Six. Eleven. Two.

My youngest son sits with his mother, bored but patient. She is praying, but he sees me looking and smiles at me. It's a goofy grin under his tousled blond hair.

He, too, is seven.

I struggle through the rest of the names and ages. I wonder how alien, how strange my son's name of "Christopher" would sound to them.

Later, I hug him, my little seven-year-old boy, and pray for the parents who can never hold their child again.

On Memorial Day, I remember, and pray never to forget.

I Listen To You Snicker

I listen to them snicker, and I wonder if they're hiding something. I want to believe that; I want to believe that they're trying to protect themselves from some pain through biting sarcasm. I'm just not sure that I can.

That night swims through my mind; I could barely walk into the mini-PX to buy the pills. I know my eyes were red from tears; I know my stare went straight through people to somewhere that didn't exist. Nobody noticed. I didn't give them much of a chance.

He talks about high-risk behaviors, about how a beer or two after work is just fine, but how a six pack or two a night is a risk behavior. Behind me, I hear an E-7 say, "Hell, that's just getting warmed up," and I remember.

I know why the guy across the hall ended up in rehab instead of me; I never made the mistake of pissing on someone's door. Other than that, there wasn't much difference between us. He had his own personal problems a thousand miles away, his family back at home. I had an infant son, a wife busy trying to smoke pot and fuck her life away, and a doomed relationship here I'd carefully constructed for myself. We both drank a lot. I was just a loner about it. I wasn't drunk when I tried; but it couldn't have helped my judgement.

I haven't told my parents yet, four years later. The closest I've come to publicly "outing" myself about this before was at a suicide prevention class I taught earlier this year.

I hear the whispered comments you make, the accusations that those people are weak, that if they can't hack it they shouldn't be in the Army, and I wonder if you know that you're talking about me. I wonder if you know that you're setting an example for your junior soldiers. I wonder if you know you're setting an example for me.

I think I'm over it now. Recently I was put under general anesthesia, and I wasn't scared. I would have been a year ago. I certainly was then.

My fingers were cold, and I had dozed. The pills were doing something, and it suddenly hit me that this was real, and the adrenaline was like a wall pushing me up, up the hill into the TMC, where I proceeded to scare the hell out of everyone I'd worked with for most of a year.

I think I managed to apologize to most of them before I left Korea.

I think about the KATUSA who blew his brains out down by the MP station that year; about the harrowing quality of his mother's wails echoing through the halls. I remember the other guy who swallowed too many pills. I hadn't liked him – and remembered that as I helped them carry the stretcher out of the second floor, as I heard the medic in the back of the ambulance say – no, scream – that he wasn't breathing.

I think about the eyes of my fellow soldiers when I came back. I think about the eyes of my son now.

I've done a lot since then, since what the psychologists decided to call a suicidal gesture. I like to think that I've helped people, that I've made a contribution to people's lives. I have a few good examples of people – NCOs and civilians – that I try to emulate, and sometimes I succeed. I hope that I affect some of my subordinates the way they – some of my earliest examples of senior NCOs – affected me.

I see you, sergeant. I see you snicker at yet another suicide prevention class, and I hope that it's a defense mechanism, that you've lost someone close to you before. That you won't let yourself think about it rationally, and joke to keep the pain at bay.

I hope... but I can't believe it.

Atomic Time

"It's okay. My watch is set to atomic time."

I knew better, yet I briefly expected to see a small nuclear generator strapped to his wrist, ticking the seconds away with radioactive precision. But no, it was just a regular plastic wristwatch (though with calculator pad and memory function) set just that morning to the most accurate time in the world. Apparently even more accurate than even the ticker clock on the Weather Channel, which disagreed with the watch by four seconds.

Normally, such a small difference would be insignificant, but this was different. This was important. Someone – nobody was quite sure who – had noticed that we were running out of year. That there were only minutes left until midnight – few seconds remained of the first (or last, depending on how you want to count) year of the millenium. The previously subdued party erupted in a frenzy of channel-flipping, trying to locate the ageless Dick Clark or, failing that, a ball dropping somewhere in the world: an effort to find an "official" countdown to chant with.

There are times when it becomes painfully obvious that I no longer live on the East Coast; New Year's is the most obvious of them. As the channels flipped by, news, after-midnight televised parties resplendent with second-rate pop icons and drunken hordes, and even the occasional rerun of a sitcom confronted us. It seemed that our only timekeeping salvation would be in the precision of a small quartz diode, only hours ago calibrated to the National Institute of Standards and Technology atomic clock, a feat made possible by technology and an Internet connection.

"We've still got three minutes," the watch-holder announced. The relief was tangible – for a moment there, we were afraid we'd missed it entirely. Paces slowed, and our final preparations continued at a more sedate pace. That is, until the bathroom door swung open, and another guest who had missed the ruckus raised their watch aloft.

"I set my watch to atomic time this morning! We've only got sixty seconds left!"

I caught sight of my reflection in the window; outside the night was dark and freezing, moonlight shone upon the snow. Behind me the ghostly reflections of people scurried, bearing hats, noisemakers, poppers, champagne. Someone was making sure the kids – collectively and safely sequestered downstairs – were on-cue and taken care of.

And we had no idea if the New Year had come yet.

Did our resolutions count yet? Did we have time for a last cigarette, a last sugary snack, a final drink? Was it time to kiss someone, or wish for someone to kiss? Should we be toasting, singing, reminding our loved ones that they were our loved ones after all? Was it time yet to start fresh, to wipe the slate clean and try to do things a little better than we had before? Nobody knew for certain – the watches disagreed with the television channels, and all of them disagreed among themselves. No ball (or Dick Clark) was visible yet, and suggestions flew back and forth. "Try CBS." "ABC! Dick Clark's on ABC!" "Headline News always has a clock!" The mood was nearly frantic – several of the timekeepers already claimed we were in the New Year. Then:

"Why don't we just say we have twenty seconds left and start counting?"

In a rollercoaster of emotion, the thought ran through our brains. Suddenly, we would decide when our New Year began. We, nobody else, would decide when to start anew, to hold ourselves to our resolutions, to love our families and remember our friends. From there, from that simple idea, realization spun outward: If it was possible to just say that the New Year began whatever time we wanted today, then we could do the same each day. Every day, every midnight, every minute could be a New Year, a new chance, a new opportunity.

The New York ball suddenly glistened upon the television in gaudy glory; someone had found it. It was a replay; Mayor Guiliani smiling as the seconds counted downward an hour ago (despite the "LIVE" blazoned in the upper-left hand corner). Dutifully, we joined in, chanting away seconds with the televised throng; distanced by thousands of miles and nearly an hour of time.

It was several minutes into the New Year, poppers popped and champagne drunk, that we noticed that the ball hadn't agreed with either of the disagreeing watches, both meticulously set to atomic time.

Twitter Fictions

Each of these stories is meant to fit into a single "tweet" - that is, 140 characters or less, including spaces.

The free-floating anxiety hovered around John's head, nagging softly, between when his mother died and when he finally called an exorcist.

My mother told me that it rained whenever someone made the baby Jesus cry. That was when I knew why I loved thunderstorms.

I think it's beautiful when your heart leaps when you see me, so no, I won't put down the car battery.

She told him to erase all traces of their affair. When she changed her mind and called back, he no longer recognized the ringtone.

Juan enjoyed the festive food at the company's diversity luncheon, but somehow it didn't make up for the "English Only" signs.

Bought Love is A Salaried Position

He screamed, running teeth-bared snarl of a child. Pre-teen, really.

The distinction was unimportant, his hundred-pound frame slamming both of us into the wall. He bit.

I remembered sex-ed classes from grade school. They talked about how much money it would cost to raise a child - impossibly high numbers for a sixth grader.

Meaningless when a girlfriend, eight years later, lies. Lies about being able to get pregnant. Lies about taking care of him when you're away serving your country, supporting your family.

The damage takes years to surface. The traumatic rage comes slow enough that you adjust, you adapt, you deal. One day, he's screaming and biting and hating. One day, he's bragging to the cops that he has a plan to kill you.

You find the hidden knife that night.

Parenthood is supposed to cost. You know that.

You never expected to pay rent.

Acknowledgements

Dedications are for those who have helped - and all have helped, even those who have hurt. Especially those who hurt.

You know who you are.

ABOUT THE AUTHOR

Steven Saus injects people with radioactivity as his day job, but only to serve the forces of good. He tries to tell lies that are absolutely true.

His work has also appeared in print in several anthologies and magazines both online and off. You can find them all at stevensaus.com, and read his blog at ideatrash.net.